ENIGMA

ENIGMA
ILLUSTRATIONS CARVED FROM WORDS

SHANE A. WAGGONER

Enigma
Copyright © 2020 by Shane A. Waggoner. All rights reserved.

No part of this publication may be reproduced, stored in a retrieval system or transmitted in any way by any means, electronic, mechanical, photocopy, recording or otherwise without the prior permission of the author except as provided by USA copyright law.

The opinions expressed by the author are not necessarily those of URLink Print and Media.

1603 Capitol Ave., Suite 310 Cheyenne, Wyoming USA 82001
1-888-980-6523 | admin@urlinkpublishing.com

URLink Print and Media is committed to excellence in the publishing industry.

Book design copyright © 2020 by URLink Print and Media. All rights reserved.

Published in the United States of America

Library of Congress Control Number: 2020904248
ISBN 978-1-64753-258-1 (Paperback)
ISBN 978-1-64753-259-8 (Digital)

21.07.20

Contents

Change 7
The Road 9
Fictive Dame 11
Omega 13
Crown of the Vile King 15
Insecurities 17
Path of Difficulties 19
Sleep 27
The Real Superheroes 29
Peace 31
Play Toy 33
Writer's Block 35
The Unexpected Visitor 37
Mankind 41
Close Minded 43
Solipsist Joe 45
Untitled.. 47

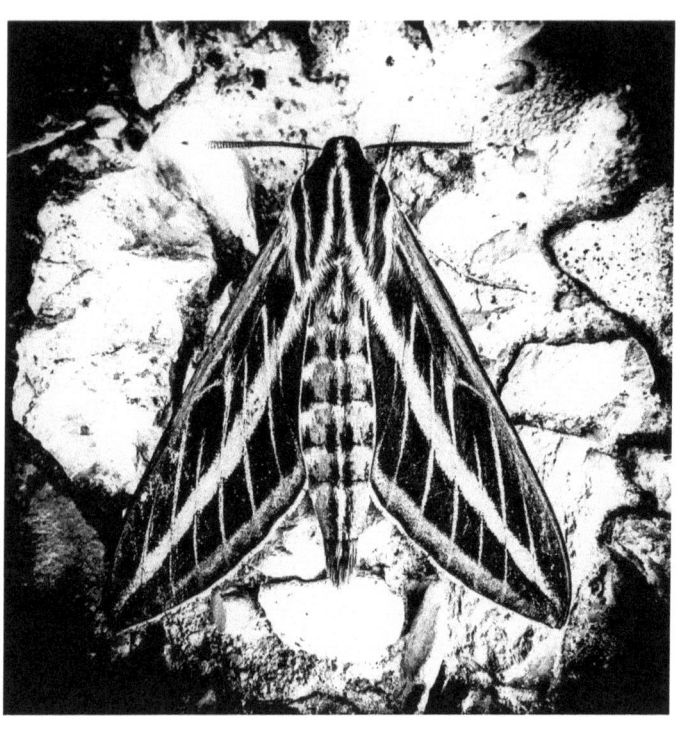

Change

The radiant sun descending upon the once vibrant skin, leaving it blooming with color and wholesome light. Its warmth liberates the exultant kept from within; a single beam of light to trounce any sentiment of fright.

Eliminating and abolishing the psychosis from inside the ruts, breaking open the door to everlasting bliss, constructing slabs to ensure it never shuts, happiness throughout, something too rare to miss.

The feeling of resolution washing over me, something the naked eye cannot see. For others, this sight of reality may not be. For me, something unreal, I dare to believe.

Now that the sun has come and gone and the colorful skin has gained back its ash, I sit and wait for the newest dawn, hoping to show off my love and not my wrath.

The Road

The road was cold, dark, and dank.
Its ashen mask told a tale of its existence.
There was a simple breeze that was almost haunting.
The trees were naked with very little bark.
There were cracks in the road,
cracks that directed a path to nowhere.
But this wasn't a road you tend to fall back on.
No.
This road had something to it.
There was a pleasant feeling that it had,
something no man could ignore.
But once a foot has placed its grips on the asphalt,
the only way to remove yourself
is to become one with the unknowns that roam there.

Fictive Dame

She walks with a sense of confidence,
she talks with a thought of intelligence.
Her hair shines like pure gold,
she had a smile that lifted spirits.
Her voice could warm the night,
her gentle words could end any fight.
So unembellished,
So impeccable,
Yet so preposterous.
What a staggering use of skin,
a face you couldn't say no to,
a trace you couldn't erase,
but who is this girl?
She is only but a myth,
a myth of high ingenuity.
She is just an ideal,
and like any ideal,
it's burned before reaching the ears of another.

Omega

This timeless reverence
lost in the ashes.
Never to be recovered,
never to see the light of day.
The corrupting passage we all walk on,
a simple ascension
has been long forsaken.

Feelings divide, can't undo,
they never tried to make it through.
Retracing the line, only a chosen few,
the sickness has made our end come true.

Somehow, we all made it here,
running from us and our perpetual fear.
Were we even meant to live?
Were we even meant to live?

The vile disease has been split on the page,
compassion for others will die in this age.
The demon in us will break from the cage,
a new wave of actions will leave us enslaved.

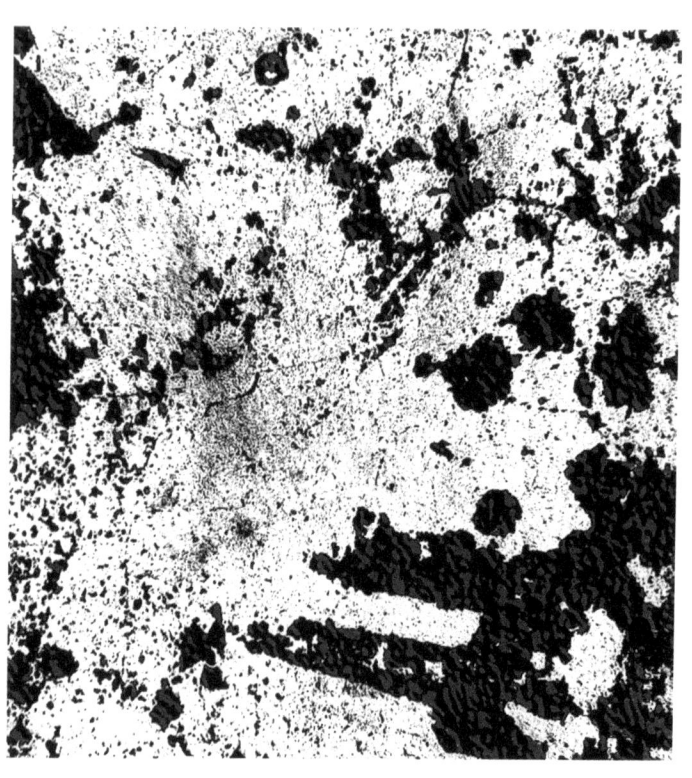

Crown of the Vile King

The Angels light has drifted along the ground,
spreading the gift without making a sound,
sent down to remove the crown
from the man making slaves of all the town.

A vile man without a beating heart,
so much hate, I don't know where to start.
His eyes are drenched in malice and lack in love.
He's been alone forever—no kids and no wife;
all by himself in his perpetual strife.

His army is too strong, revolt is not in question.
Freedom is no longer in the people's possession.
Families being ripped apart, severed,
a content lifestyle is now over.

His evil intentions start to flee.
The blackened eyes now able to see.
His once peaceful empire now an unstoppable hell,
a realization that not all is well.

The light pierces through the darkness,
allowing the evaporation of sadness.
The people's bliss starts to regenerate,
as the crown of the vile king disintegrates.

Insecurities

I'm a block in your mind,
I'm the delay of your success,
I'm a lightless pit controlling your life,
I'm the tear-jerking, rage-inducing uncontrollable mess.

You hate me to death,
you waste every breath,
you allow me to feed,
you forget what you need.

The need to understand change,
the need to believe in yourself,
the need to be patient,
the need to overcome stress.

You are different,
you are unique,
you are no one else,
you are perfect.

Path of Difficulties

They lash, beat, and batter him bloody.
His life is empty; he's left with nobody.
Everything that goes great and right
gets obliterated in the dead of night.
The school never bats a finger,
as the hate and torture still lingers.
His family doesn't care;
life's too hard to bare.
The stars do not align for Alex Smith.
He sits at home and weeps.
Inside his head, the madness slowly creeps.
He tries to be friendly,
he tries to be kind.
But they only have one thing in mind:
to abuse and harm Alex Smith.
His tears begin to pour
as they deliver more.
Every muscle sore
from the beatings he absorbs.

As a new day approaches,
something new arises.

Alex is confronted by a female,
a beautiful dame dressed elegantly.
She looks him in the eye and says, "Hello."
He stutters as he tries to greet her back.
She smiles at him and laughs.
Alex generates a smile of his own,
something he hasn't done in a great while.
She asks if he is free tonight.
He replies slowly with "I always am."
Alex is told to meet her on the football field at night.
He hesitantly asks why.
Her response is "You'll see."
He smiles and agrees to her demands.

As night fall covers the sky,
Alex is still wondering why,
why the football field at night?
He prays it will go all right.
Sitting on his bedside, he prays,
praying for many wonderful ways
that this night could turn out.

As he starts his journey to the field,
he grows anxious.
He gets there, and there she is,
the prettiest girl he's ever laid eyes on.
He slowly makes his way to her.
They meet on the fifty-year line.
Conversation after conversation
and Alex's beautiful girl, without hesitation,

asks him to close his eyes.
She grabs his shoulders and shortens the distance.
Alex starts an uncontrollable shake
as they almost touch lips.
Alex feels a sharp pain in his hips.
He was kicked by a steel-toed boot.
Jocks stand over his aching body
before Alex could react.
They began to attack
all while Alex is being abused.
The woman who he thought was pretty and kind
was yelling "Hit him harder" off to the side.
Alex couldn't tell if tears or blood
ran down his wounded face.
The beatings stopped quickly
when out of the night, a yell was heard.
The coach came sprinting on the field,
quickly the others ran away.
The man stopped to help Alex.
He lay drowning in his own blood.
His body twitched and shook.
The man placed Alex in his arms,
loaded him in his truck,
and hurried to the emergency room.
The staff began work rapidly,
fixing his body from the damage.

As night passed the town,
Alex lay in the hospital bed.
Suddenly, his eyes opened.

The coach walked in.
Alex's eyes widened.
He told Alex of the events of last night.
Before Alex could make a move,
a nurse entered the room.
She changed his IV bag,
checked his blood pressure,
and told him to relax.
"Don't touch that thing in your neck."
The nurse directed toward Alex.
"It's basically your life source."
She exits the room.
Alex begins to rest his eyes.

He's awaken by a light tap.
The coach appears in his vision.
He tells Alex not to worry and that he'll be back.
Alex nods and looks up.
After a short while of silence,
Alex reaches for his neck,
grabbing ahold of the tube.
He slowly starts to pull,
tired of the torture
done with the abuse.
Alex didn't just want peace,
he needed it.
He kept pulling.
Until suddenly, he remembered,
remembered wise words he was given,
given by an old educator of his:

Suicide is never the answer.
There's a better, more efficient manner.
It eliminates the possibility of change.
Rising above the situation is much better.
Show the world you will not give up;
you control yourself,
you set your own destiny.
Survive and learn from the difficult years
to be able to appreciate the good ones.
 Alex stopped pulling,
his hand eased its way back to his side.
The coach came back in,
telling Alex he had one more night to rest
and he'd be back tomorrow.

Morning rolled around the corner.
Alex awoke to find the coach talking to the nurse.
They looked and saw him awake,
informing him that he could go.
Alex smiled in relief.
Exiting the hospital, the coach asked,
"Where do you live?"
Alex shrugged his shoulders.
"Anywhere."
Coach was stunned at that response.
He gave Alex a hug.
Leaving to get the car, he had Alex wait.
They left the hospital.
It was a drive filled with silence.
Alex, sore all over, looked out the window.

The car stopped outside a middle-class house.
Both men stepped out.
Coach led the way.
He informed Alex he could stay with him.
Alex agreed without hesitation.
Coach's wife, Mrs. Green, prepared the guest room.
Alex went up there to cry tears of joy.
This to Alex meant everything.

Years later, Alex is on his own,
with a wonderful wife and a beautiful son,
who he gives all his love to.
Life turned out amazing for Alex
all because he made the right choice,
rejected the idea of giving up,
and walked through the difficult path
to emerge onto the better, brighter path.

Sleep

Life was beautiful.
Love was easily found.
Pain was snuffed.
Passion was kept.
Negativity was lost.
Negligence was sent away.
Sorrow was destroyed.
Simplicity was everywhere.
Arrogance was never seen.
Assumptions was not allowed.
Inchoation was joyful.
Invulnerability was in everything.
Trust was believable.
Time was on our side.
Then I awoke.

The Real Superheroes

They paved my roads.
They constructed my walls.
They'll forever live in my memories.
Men who built a whole family,
built greatness with their hands,
respected and loved forever.
Wishing I could have a moment,
a moment to talk, laugh, and live with you,
and be your grandson one last time.
I'll always cherish my time with you.
I hope you can see the man I am today.
I try to model after you two,
follow the footsteps of legends
whose legacies will carry on forever.

I miss and love you both.

Peace

As I gaze through the forest,
I feel the wind upon my face
and find rhythm to nature,
allowing its beauty to take hold of me,
remaining calm and focused,
focused on the peacefulness.
The light finds me through the trees,
shining down on me,
adding warmth through my body,
helping me find halcyon.

Play Toy

The eyes remained locked on her.
She didn't know what to do.
It was big and covered with fur.
It was her it was coming to.

Cold, still, and drenched in fear,
she thought her end was closing near.
Step-by-step, its distance closed.
Why was it her it choose?

Fangs and claws glistening with blood,
its feet drowning in mud.
Her screams growing louder,
her fate nearly sealed.

The alley way filled with noise.
Face-to-face they stood
until a series of strikes.

Writer's Block

The emptiness in my mind,
the hollow space inside,
stealing all my time,
denying me a sign.
A blank canvas sits and waits
for something ready to create.
The pin sits patiently,
begging to be used,
yet now rendered obsolete.
For the time being,
he weeps alone
until the time comes
and inspiration sparks.

The Unexpected Visitor

On a cold, wet night, when the town was still and the streets were clear, a police station lobby laid empty. The lady was running the front window nearly falling asleep until two police officers walked through the entrance doors.

"Tonight stinks, there's nothing going on," said one of the officers. They walked over to the lady at the window. They began chatting with one another about some of the crazier people locked away in the station.

"I heard she ate her own feces," said the lady. The conversation quickly jumped to how slow the night was going, how usually the calls are coming in at an alarming rate. The two officers were confused as what to do since they don't normally sit and wait for this long on a call. Driving to the station was an old truck with chipped paint. It was the only one located on the street. It soon pulled into a parking lot. The truck stopped, and the door opened. A man stepped out of the cab. It was too dark to see any features of his face. He reached across the cab and grabbed an object out of the passenger seat.

The cops still sat in the lobby conversing with each other. The man was walking toward the building. The building was the police station. He entered the first set of doors and then through the final set of doors. The cops and the lady looked toward the visitor. They were baffled at what they saw. The man was wearing overalls with a white long sleeve shirt, boots, and leather gloves. All these garments were soaked in blood. In his left hand was an axe. It was also covered in blood. The cops were too shocked to do anything. The man dropped the axe and fell to his knees. His face held a dazed look, and his eyes were focused on the bloody axe. The cops quickly ran over and cuffed him. They dragged him to the back of the station.

A silent night turned into a bloodbath for an unfortunate pair of souls.

Mankind

The evolution of man has spiraled into a giant ball of nothingness, ready to implode. The answers are locked away in a vault. Ready to escape, but alas, the keys are lost. We run in terror only to see what we didn't see before. We caused this. Our actions melted the key. Our actions left us this way. We've gone too far. Will we ever return to the way things were?

Close Minded

Simplistic minds,
close-minded souls,
concrete beliefs,
bolted skulls.
Nothing new,
same old thing.
Don't waste your breath.
Nothing left.
Zero change,
they're all deranged.
Love to hate.
Those who hear
all the thoughts
from those involved.
Close minded then,
close minded now,
close minded 'til death,
such a waste of the human mind.

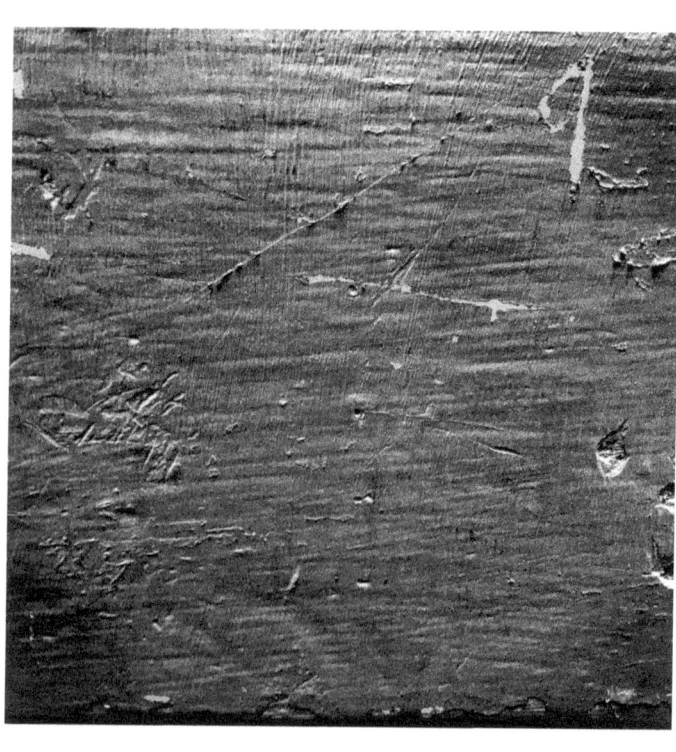

Solipsist Joe

The corridors are blank empty walls,
yet to be smitten by my own blood.

Forbidding shadows stalk 'neath
the ashes of the fallen sun.

The banshee screams until her lungs
give way unto the temperamental flood.

Every nightmare foreshadowed, but never heeded.
The river ran barren as I screamed and pleaded.

The haunted gather 'round the tomb
to mark me as enemy.

For now it is I who shall suffer

In my own eternity.

Untitled

Man's gift is the aptitude to be true
In diminutive times, thy will begin to slew

An upward force of confusion and agony
Constructing walls built from greed and vanity

The mortal face swallowed by the unforgiving mask
Melting in the glory in which we think we bask

Follow the leader until execution
Drowning in a sea of mass dilution

Put a bullet in the head of our gift
Stray too far, and you'll neglect the shift.

www.ingramcontent.com/pod-product-compliance
Ingram Content Group UK Ltd.
Pitfield, Milton Keynes, MK11 3LW, UK
UKHW022208230426
12048UKWH00016BA/727